I Am Po

by Sean King   **illustrated by Julie Durrell**

Harcourt

Orlando   Boston   Dallas   Chicago   San Diego

Visit *The Learning Site!*

www.harcourtschool.com

ISBN 0-15-325471-8

16 17 18 19 20 985 10 09 08 07

Ordering Options
ISBN 0-15-325468-8 (Collection)
ISBN 0-15-326549-3 (package of 5)

I am Pat.

I am a pig.

I am a dog.

I am a bug.

I am a fox.

I am a cat.

Meow! Meow!